THE BRAVE
BEAST

CHRIS JUDGE

For Andrew, Ciara, Emma and Simon

Other books by Chris Judge

The Lonely Beast
The Great Explorer

First published in Great Britain in 2013 by Andersen Press Ltd., 20 Vauxhall Bridge Road, London SW1V 2SA.
Published in Australia by Random House Australia Pty., Level 3, 100 Pacific Highway, North Sydney, NSW 2060.
Text and illustrations copyright © Chris Judge, 2013. The rights of Chris Judge to be identified as the author and illustrator
of this work have been asserted by him in accordance with the Copyright, Designs and Patents Act, 1988.
All rights reserved. Printed and bound in Singapore by Tien Wah Press.
10 9 8 7 6 5 4 3 2 1 ... Cataloguing in Publication Data available.

9030 00003 3148 7

The Beast was resting
in his peaceful garden
after a long day's work . . .

... when he heard the noise of an aeroplane coming in to land.

"Beast, Beast, we need your help!"
said the pilot, rushing from the plane.

WARRROOOOOOOOOOOO!!!

"Something terrible has happened! There's a scary noise coming from the middle of our island.

WARRROOOOOOOOOOOOOOOOOOOOO!!!

Everyone is so frightened that they have left!

It must be a truly ferocious monster to make so much noise. Will you help us to get rid of it, please?"

The Beast felt very scared.

But he decided to be brave and help the islanders.

So they both boarded the plane . . .

. . . and off they set!

When they reached the island, the pilot was too scared to land,

so the Beast bravely leapt from the plane . . .

...and swam ashore.

SPLASH!

He made his way towards the village.

"Hello?" he called out nervously, but it was deserted.

He walked towards the middle of the island . . .

until he reached a deep, dark tunnel in the cliff.

...he reached the far side of the island.

He made his way through a spooky forest,

which got thicker . . .

. . . and thicker . . .

. . . until it got very dark.

WARRROOOOOOOOOOOOO

WHRRRUUUUUOOOUUUUOOOUUUUO

The Beast was so scared
that he ran round and round
the forest in fright.

OOOOUUOUOUOUOOOOOOUUU!!!

At last, he found a gigantic
tree to hide behind . . .

...but the noise was coming from right behind it!

Cautiously, the Beast edged his way towards it.

Plucking up all his courage, the Beast peered
round the trunk and saw . . .

...a tiny little bird.

"Surely it wasn't you making all that noise?"
asked the Beast in disbelief.

The little bird explained that he had got lost
and had landed on the island.

"I'm sorry that I made so much noise
and frightened away the islanders,"
he sobbed, "but I was very lonely
and couldn't stop crying."

The Beast went back to the village and phoned the pilot to
let him know it was safe for the islanders to return.

"Don't worry," said the Beast. "I am sure that the islanders
will look after you, when they hear what has happened."

The islanders were very
happy to return home.

Relieved that the Beast had solved the mystery,
the islanders were only too happy to invite the
little bird to live with them.

They gave him a job in the lighthouse, and he was thrilled as it made him feel very important.

The grateful islanders waved the brave Beast goodbye and said that he was welcome to come and stay any time.

But the Beast was very happy to be home again in his peaceful garden . . .

... until his next
adventure, at least.